EARTH DAY, BIRTHDAY!

written by **Maureen Wright**   illustrated by **Violet Kim**

APRIL

two lions

two lions

All rights reserved
Amazon Publishing

Attn: Amazon Children's Publishing, P.O. Box 400818, Las Vegas, NV 89140
www.amazon.com/amazonchildrenspublishing

Library of Congress Cataloging-in-Publication Data

Wright, Maureen, 1961-
Earth Day, birthday! / by Maureen Wright ; illustrated by Violet Kim. —
1st ed.
    p. cm.
    Summary: When Monkey proclaims that it is his birthday, all the other jungle
animals protest, claiming instead that it is Earth Day and telling Monkey what
he should do to honor this special day.
    ISBN 978-0-7614-6109-8 (hardcover) — ISBN 978-0-7614-6110-4 (ebook)
    [1. Stories in rhyme. 2. Jungle animals—Fiction. 3. Environmental protection—
Fiction. 4. Earth Day—Fiction. 5. Birthdays—Fiction.] I. Kim, Violet, ill. II. Title.
    PZ8.3.W9363Ear 2012
                                      [E]—dc23   2011016395

The illustrations are rendered in paper, photographs, and colored pencils.

Printed in China

Text copyright © 2012
by Maureen Wright
Illustrations copyright © 2012
by Violet Kim

Book design by Vera Soki
Editor: Margery Cuyler

In loving memory of
Ed and Grace Wright
—M. W.

Dedicated to my family
& Judy, for their great
support of my art
—V. K.

Deep within the jungle green,
the biggest lion ever seen,
stood before his friends and said,
"Happy Earth Day!"

Deep within the jungle green,
the silliest monkey ever seen,
swung upon a branch and said,
"It's not Earth Day! It's my birthday!"

The elephant shook her wrinkled head
and stomped her foot like a bag of lead.
She turned to Monkey and loudly said,
"It's Earth Day, not your birthday!

Let's plant a row of tiny trees,
plow a garden for beans and peas.
Grab a shovel, get a hoe!
Hurry up, it's time to go!"

Deep within the jungle green,
the silliest monkey ever seen,
twirled his tail and proudly said,
"It's not Earth Day! It's my birthday!"

The lumpy, bumpy crocodile
watched the monkey for awhile.
He answered with a toothy smile,
"It's Earth Day, not your birthday!"

MAKE THE
WORLD A
PRETTIER PLACE

"Let's pick up papers off the ground.
There's lots of litter—look around!
Collect the garbage that you see.
Stick it in a bag for me!"

Deep within the jungle green,
the silliest monkey ever seen,
ate a banana and proudly said,
"It's not Earth Day! It's my birthday!"

The tall giraffe complained, "Oh, dear!
I see we have a problem here.
Let me make this very clear . . .
It's Earth Day, not your birthday!"

"We'll do our part to clean the land . . .
recycle bottles, glasses, cans.
Come on, my friends, I'll lead the way!
Let's recycle every day!"

Deep within the jungle green,
the silliest monkey ever seen,
rubbed his belly and proudly said,
"It's not Earth Day! It's my birthday!"

Hippo opened his mouth up wide
on the muddy riverside.
He turned to Monkey and loudly cried,
"It's Earth Day, not your birthday!"

"Let's take our cloth bags to the store . . .
buy three pineapples, maybe four!
We'll use our cloth bags every time
to shop for coconuts and limes."

USE CLOTH BAGS
INSTEAD OF PLASTIC

Deep within the jungle green,
the silliest monkey ever seen,
shimmied up a tree and said,
"It's not Earth Day! It's my birthday!"

Snake slithered through the leaves up high,
as the monkey scampered by.
She raised her head and said, "Oh my!
It's Earth Day, not your birthday!"

"Let's go start a compost bin . . .
toss our rotten garbage in!
Watch me and I'll show you how.
We'll get started on it now!"

Deep within the jungle green,
the silliest monkey ever seen,
jumped around and proudly said,
"It's not Earth Day! It's my birthday!"

He whispered in the lion's ear,
"Don't you know my birthday's here?"

Lion roared back,

"Give me a break!

I've heard ALL that I can take!
No matter what we do or say,
you think it is your special day!"

"But it *is*!" said Monkey. "Can't you see?
Here's my mom with a cake for me!"

The lion gasped, "I made a mistake.
Please share your yummy birthday cake!"

"Of course!" said Monkey with a shout.
"But first I'll blow these candles out."